HORRID HENRY'S CHRISTMAS

Meet HORRID HENRY
the laugh-out-loud
worldwide sensation!

···

★ Over 15 million copies sold in 27
   countries and counting

★ #1 chapter book series in the UK

★ Francesca Simon is the only American
   author to ever win the Galaxy British
   Book Awards Children's Book of the year
   (past winners include J.K. Rowling, Philip
   Pullman, and Eoin Colfer).

"Horrid Henry is a fabulous antihero…**a modern comic classic.**" —*Guardian*

"**Wonderfully appealing to girls and boys alike**, a precious rarity at this age." —Judith Woods, *Times*

• •

"The best children's comic writer." —Amanda Craig, Times

• •

"**I love the Horrid Henry books by Francesca Simon.** They have lots of funny bits in. And Henry always gets into trouble!" —Mia, age 6, *BBC Learning Is Fun*

"My two boys love this book, and **I have actually had tears running down my face and had to stop reading because of laughing so hard.**" —T. Franklin, Parent

"**It's easy to see why Horrid Henry is the bestselling character for five- to eight-year-olds.**" —*Liverpool Echo*

"Francesca Simon's truly horrific little boy is **a monstrously enjoyable creation**. Parents love them because Henry makes their own little darlings seem like angels." —*Guardian Children's Books Supplement*

"I have tried out the Horrid Henry books with groups of children as a parent, as a babysitter, and as a teacher. **Children love to either hear them read aloud or to read them themselves.**" —Danielle Hall, Teacher

"A flicker of recognition must pass through most teachers and parents when they read Horrid Henry. **There's a tiny bit of him in all of us**." —Nancy Astee, *Child Education*

"**As a teacher...it's great to get a series of books my class loves.** They go mad for Horrid Henry." —A teacher

"**Henry is a beguiling hero who has entranced millions of reluctant readers.**" —*Herald*

....

"An absolutely fantastic series and surely a winner with all children. Long live Francesca Simon and her brilliant books! More, more please!"   —A parent

....

"**The humor will have you laughing your pants off.**" —Examiner.com

"**Horrid Henry certainly lives up to his name, and his antics are everything you hope your own child will avoid—which is precisely why younger children so enjoy these tales.**" —*Independent on Sunday*

"Henry might be unbelievably naughty, totally wicked, and utterly horrid, but **he is frequently credited with converting the most reluctant readers into enthusiastic ones**...superb in its simplicity." —*Liverpool Echo*

Horrid Henry by Francesca Simon

HORRID HENRY'S CHRISTMAS

Francesca Simon
Illustrated by Tony Ross

sourcebooks
jabberwocky

Text © Francesca Simon 2006
Internal illustrations © Tony Ross 2006
Cover illustration © Tony Ross 2008
Cover and internal design © 2009 by Sourcebooks, Inc.

Published by Sourcebooks Jabberwocky, an imprint of Sourcebooks, Inc.
P.O. Box 4410, Naperville, Illinois 60567–4410
(630) 961–3900
Fax: (630) 961–2168
www.jabberwockykids.com

Originally published in Great Britain in 2006 by Orion Children's Books.

Cataloging-in-Publication Data is on file with the publisher.

Source of Production: RR Donnelley, Crawfordsville, IN, USA
Date of Production: May 2017
Run Number: POD

Printed and bound in the United States of America.
POD 10 9 8 7 6 5

For the one and only
Miranda Richardson

CONTENTS

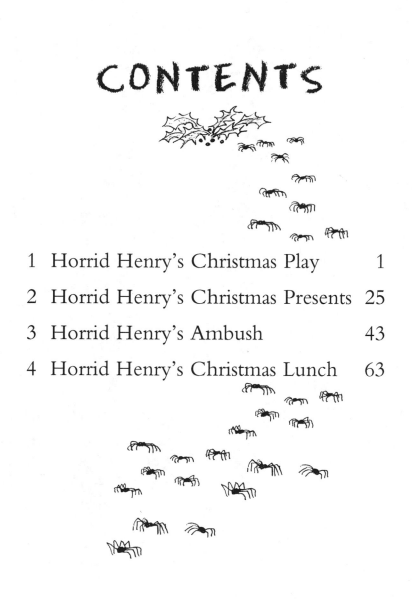

HORRID HENRY'S CHRISTMAS PLAY

A cold dark day in November
(37 days till Christmas)

Horrid Henry slumped on the carpet and willed the clock to go faster. Only five more minutes to home time! Already Henry could taste those chips he'd be sneaking from the cupboard.

Miss Battle-Axe droned on about school lunches (yuck), the new drinking fountain blah blah blah, math homework blah blah blah, the school Christmas play blah blah . . . what? Did Miss Battle-Axe say . . . Christmas play? Horrid Henry sat up.

"This is a brand-new play with singing and dancing," continued Miss Battle-Axe. "And both the older and the younger children are taking part this year."

Singing! Dancing! Showing off in front of the whole school! Years ago, when Henry was in kindergarten, he'd played eighth sheep in the nativity play and had snatched the baby from the manger and refused to hand him back. Henry hoped Miss Battle-Axe wouldn't remember.

Because Henry had to play the lead. He had to. Who else but Henry could be an all-singing, all-dancing Joseph?

"I want to be Mary!" shouted every girl in the class.

"I want to be a wise man!" shouted Rude Ralph.

"I want to be a sheep!" shouted Anxious Andrew.

"I want to be Joseph!" shouted Horrid Henry.

"No, me!" shouted Jazzy Jim.

"Me!" shouted Brainy Brian.

"Quiet!" shrieked Miss Battle-Axe. "I'm the director, and my decision about who will act which part is final. I've cast the play as follows: Margaret. You will be Mary." She handed her a thick script.

Moody Margaret whooped with joy. All the other girls glared at her.

"Susan, front legs of the donkey; Linda, hind legs; cows, Fiona and Clare. Blades of grass—" Miss Battle-Axe continued assigning parts.

Pick me for Joseph, pick me for Joseph, Horrid Henry begged silently. Who better than the best actor in the school to play the starring part?

"I'm a sheep, I'm a sheep, I'm a

3

beautiful sheep!" warbled Singing Soraya.

"I'm a shepherd!" beamed Jolly Josh.

"I'm an angel," trilled Magic Martha.

"I'm a blade of grass," sobbed Weepy William.

"Joseph will be played by—"

"ME!" screamed Henry.

"Me!" screamed New Nick, Greedy Graham, Dizzy Dave, and Aerobic Al.

"—Peter," said Miss Battle-Axe. "From Miss Lovely's class."

Horrid Henry felt as if he'd been slugged in the stomach. Perfect Peter?

His *younger* brother? Perfect Peter gets the starring part?

"It's not fair!" howled Horrid Henry.

Miss Battle-Axe glared at him.

"Henry, you're—" Miss Battle-Axe consulted her list. Please not a blade of grass, please not a blade of grass, prayed Horrid Henry, shrinking. That would be just like Miss Battle-Axe, to humiliate him. Anything but that—

"—the innkeeper."

The innkeeper! Horrid Henry sat up, beaming. How stupid he'd been: the *innkeeper* must be the starring part. Henry could see himself now, polishing glasses, throwing darts, pouring out big foaming Fizzywizz drinks to all his happy customers while singing a song about the joys of innkeeping. Then he'd get into a nice long argument about why there was no room at the inn, and finally, the chance to slam the door in Moody

Margaret's face after he'd pushed her away. Wow. Maybe he'd even get a second song. "Ninety-Nine Bottles of Pop on the Wall" would fit right into the story: he'd sing and dance while knocking his less talented classmates off a wall. Wouldn't that be fun!

Miss Battle-Axe handed a page to Henry. "Your script," she said.

Henry was puzzled. Surely there were some pages missing?

He read:

(Joseph knocks. The innkeeper opens the door.)

JOSEPH: Is there any room at the inn?
INNKEEPER: No.

(The innkeeper shuts the door.)

Horrid Henry turned over the page.
It was blank. He held it up to the light.

There was no secret writing. That was it.

His entire part was one line. One stupid puny line. Not even a line, a word. "No."

Where was his song? Where was his dance with the bottles and the guests at the inn? How could he, Horrid Henry, the best actor in the class (and indeed, the world) be given just one word in the school play? Even the donkeys got a song.

Worse, after he said his *one* word, Perfect Peter and Moody Margaret got to yack for hours about mangers and wise men and shepherds and sheep, and then sing a duet, while he, Henry, hung around behind the hay with the blades of grass.

It was so unfair!

He should be the star of the show, not his stupid worm of a brother. Why on earth was Peter cast as Joseph anyway? He was a terrible actor. He couldn't sing, he just squeaked like a squished toad. And why was Margaret playing Mary? Now she'd never stop bragging and swaggering.

AAARRRRGGGGHHHH!

"Isn't it exciting!" said Mom.

"Isn't it thrilling!" said Dad. "Our little boy, the star of the show."

"Well done, Peter," said Mom.

"We're so proud of you," said Dad.

Perfect Peter smiled modestly.

"Of course I'm not *really* the star," he said, "Everyone's important, even little parts like the blades of grass and the innkeeper."

Horrid Henry pounced. He was a Great White shark lunging for the kill.

"AAAARRRRGGGHH!" squealed Peter. "Henry bit me!"

"Henry! Don't be horrid!" snapped Mom.

"Henry! Go to your room!" snapped Dad.

Horrid Henry stomped upstairs and slammed the door. How could he bear the humiliation of playing the innkeeper when Peter was the star? He'd just have to force Peter to switch roles with him. Henry was sure he could find a way to persuade Peter, but persuading Miss Battle-Axe was a different matter. Miss Battle-Axe had a mean, horrible way of never doing what Henry wanted.

Maybe he could trick Peter into leaving the show. Yes! And then nobly offer to replace him.

But unfortunately, there was no guarantee Miss Battle-Axe would give Henry Peter's role. She'd probably just replace Peter with Goody-Goody Gordon. He was stuck.

And then Horrid Henry had a brilliant, spectacular idea. Why hadn't he thought of this before? If he couldn't play a bigger part, he'd just have to make his part bigger. For instance, he could *scream* "No." *That* would get a reaction. Or he could bellow "No," and then hit Joseph.

10

I'm an angry innkeeper, thought Horrid
Henry, and I hate guests coming to my
inn. Certainly smelly ones like Joseph.
Or he could shout "No," hit Joseph,
then rob him. I'm a robber innkeeper,
thought Henry. Or, I'm a robber
pretending to be an innkeeper. That
would liven up the play a bit. Maybe
he could be a French robber innkeeper,
shout "*Non*," and rob Mary and Joseph.
Or he was a French robber *pirate* innkeeper, so he could shout "*Non*," tie
Mary and Joseph up, and make them
walk the plank.
Hmmm,
thought
Horrid
Henry.
Maybe
my
part
won't be

so small. After all, the innkeeper *was* the most important character.

December 12th
(only 13 more days till Christmas)

Rehearsals had been going on forever. Horrid Henry spent most of his time slumping in a chair. He'd never seen such a boring play. Naturally he'd done everything he could to improve it.

"Can't I add a dance?" asked Henry.

"No," snapped Miss Battle-Axe.

"Can't I add a teeny-weeny-little song?" Henry pleaded.

"No!" said Miss Battle-Axe.

"But how does the innkeeper *know* there's no room?"

said Henry. "I think I should—"

Miss Battle-Axe glared at him with her red eyes.

"One more word from you, Henry, and you'll change places with Linda," snapped Miss Battle-Axe. "Blades of grass, let's try again . . ."

Eeek! An innkeeper with one word was infinitely better than being invisible as the hind legs of a donkey. Still—it was so unfair. He was only trying to help.

December 22nd
(only 3 more days till Christmas!)

Showtime! Not a dish towel was to be found in any local shop. Moms and dads had been up all night frantically sewing costumes. Now the waiting and the rehearsing were over.

Everyone lined up on stage behind the curtain. Peter and Margaret waited on the side to make their big entrance as Mary and Joseph.

"Isn't it exciting, Henry, being in a real play?" whispered Peter.

"NO," snarled Henry.

"Places, everyone, for the opening song," hissed Miss Battle-Axe. "Now remember, don't worry if you make a little mistake: just carry on and no one will notice."

"But I still think I should have an

argument with Mary and Joseph about whether there's room," said Henry. "Shouldn't I at least check to see—"

"No!" snapped Miss Battle-Axe, glaring at him. "If I hear another peep from you, Henry, you will sit behind the bales of hay and Jim will play your part. Blades of grass! Line up with the donkeys! Sheep! Get ready to baaa . . . Bert! Are you a sheep or a blade of grass?"

"I dunno," said Beefy Bert.

Mrs. Oddbod went to the front of the stage. "Welcome everyone, moms and dads, boys and girls, to our new Christmas play, a little different from previous years. We hope you all enjoy a brand-new show!"

Miss Battle-Axe started the CD player. The music played. The curtain rose. The audience stamped and cheered. Stars twinkled. Cows mooed. Horses neighed. Sheep baa'ed. Cameras flashed.

Horrid Henry stood in the wings and watched the shepherds do their Highland dance. He still hadn't decided for sure how he was going to play his part. There were so many possibilities. It was so hard to choose.

Finally, Henry's big moment arrived.

He strode across the stage and waited behind the closed inn door for Mary and Joseph.

Knock!

Knock!
Knock!

The innkeeper stepped forward and opened the door. There was Moody Margaret, simpering away as Mary, and Perfect Peter looking full of himself as Joseph.

"Is there any room at the inn?" asked Joseph.

Good question, thought Horrid Henry. His mind was blank. He'd thought of so many great things he *could* say that what he was *supposed* to say had just gone straight out of his head.

"Is there any room at the inn?" repeated Joseph loudly.

"Yes," said the innkeeper. "Come on in."

Joseph looked at Mary.

Mary looked at Joseph.

The audience murmured.

Oops, thought Horrid Henry. Now he remembered. He'd been supposed to say no. Oh well, the show must go on.

The innkeeper grabbed Mary and Joseph's sleeves and yanked them through the door. "Come on in, I haven't got all day."

" . . . But . . . but . . . the inn's *full*," said Mary.

"No it isn't," said the innkeeper.

"Is too."

"Is not. It's my inn and I should know. This is the best inn in Bethlehem, we've got TVs and beds, and—" the innkeeper paused for a moment. What *did* inns have in them? "—and computers!"

Mary glared at the innkeeper.

The innkeeper glared at Mary.

Miss Battle-Axe gestured frantically from the wings.

"This inn looks full to me," said Mary firmly. "Come on Joseph, let's go to the stable."

"Oh, don't go there, you'll get fleas," said the innkeeper.

"So?" said Mary.

"I love fleas," said Joseph weakly.

"And it's full of manure."

"So are you," snapped Mary.

"Don't be horrid, Mary," said the inn-keeper severely. "Now sit down and

19

rest your weary bones and I'll sing you a song." And the innkeeper started singing:

Ninety-nine bottles of pop on the wall,
Ninety-nine bottles of pop on the wall,
And if one of those bottles should happen
to fall—"

"OOOHHH!" moaned Mary. "I'm having the baby."

"Can't you wait till I've finished my song?" snapped the innkeeper.

"NO!" bellowed Mary.

Miss Battle-Axe drew her hand across her throat.

Henry ignored her. After all, the show must go on.

"Come on, Joseph," interrupted Mary. "We're going to the stable."

"OK," said Joseph.

"You're making a big mistake," said the innkeeper. "We've got satellite TV and . . . "

Miss Battle-Axe ran onstage.

"Thank you, innkeeper, your other guests need you now," said Miss Battle-Axe, grabbing him by the collar.

"Merry Christmas!" shrieked Horrid Henry as she yanked him offstage.

There was a very long silence.

"Bravo!" yelled Moody Margaret's deaf aunt.

Mom and Dad weren't sure what to do. Should they clap or run away to a place where no one knew them?

Mom clapped.

Dad hid his face in his hands.

"Do you think anyone noticed?" whispered Mom.

Dad looked at Mrs. Oddbod's grim face. He sank down in his chair. Maybe one day he would learn how to make himself invisible.

"But what was I *supposed* to do?" said Horrid Henry afterward in Mrs. Oddbod's office. "It's not *my* fault I forgot my line. Miss Battle-Axe said not to worry if we made a mistake and just to carry on."

Could he help it if a star was born?

HORRID HENRY'S CHRISTMAS PRESENTS

December 23rd
(Just two more days to go!!!)

Horrid Henry sat by the Christmas tree and stuffed himself full of the special candy he'd swiped from the special Christmas Day stash when Mom and Dad weren't looking. After his triumph in the school Christmas play, Horrid Henry was feeling delighted with himself and with the world.

Granny and Grandpa, his grown-up cousins Pimply Paul and Prissy Polly, and

their baby, Vomiting Vera, were coming
to spend Christmas. Whoopee, thought
Horrid Henry, because they'd all have
to bring *him* presents. Thankfully, Rich
Aunt Ruby and Stuck-Up Steve weren't
coming. They were off skiing. Henry
hadn't forgotten the dreadful lime green
cardigan Aunt Ruby had given him last
year. And as much as he hated cousin
Polly, anyone was better than Stuck-Up
Steve, even someone who squealed all
the time and had a baby who threw up
on everyone.

Mom dashed into the living room,
wearing a flour-covered apron and
looking frantic. Henry choked down
his mouthful of candy.

"Right, who wants to decorate the
tree?" said Mom. She held out a
cardboard box brimming with tinsel and
gold and silver and blue baubles.

"Me!" said Henry.

"Me!" said Peter.

Horrid Henry dashed to the box and scooped up as many shiny ornaments as he could.

"I want to put on the gold baubles," said Henry.

"I want to put on the tinsel," said Peter.

"Keep away from my side of the tree," hissed Henry.

"You don't have a side," said Peter.

"Do too."

"Do not," said Peter.

"I want to put on the tinsel *and* the baubles," said Henry.

"But I want to do the tinsel," said Peter.

"Tough," said Henry, draping Peter in tinsel.

"Mooom!" wailed Peter. "Henry's hogging all the decorations! And he's putting tinsel on me."

"Don't be horrid, Henry," said Mom. "Share with your brother."

Peter carefully wrapped blue tinsel around the lower branches.

"Don't put it there," said Henry, yanking it off. Trust Peter to ruin his beautiful plan.

"MOOOM!" wailed Peter.

"He's wrecking my design," screeched Henry. "He doesn't know how to decorate a tree."

"But I wanted it there!" protested Peter. "Leave my tinsel alone."

"You leave my stuff alone then," said Henry.

"He wrecked my design!" shrieked Henry and Peter.

28

"Stop fighting, both of you!" shrieked
Mom.

"He started it!" screamed Henry.

"Did not!"

"Did too!"

"That's enough," said Mom. "Now,
whose turn is it to put the fairy on top?"

"I don't want to have that stupid
fairy," wailed Horrid Henry. "I want to
have Terminator Gladiator instead."

"No," said Peter. "I want the fairy.
We always have the fairy."

"Terminator!"

"Fairy!"

"TERMINATOR!"

"FAIRY!"

Slap Slap

"WAAAAAAA!"

"We're having the fairy," said Mom firmly, "and *I'll* put it on the tree."

"NOOOOOO!" screamed Henry. "Why can't we do what I want to do? I never get to have what I want."

"Liar!" whimpered Peter.

"I've had enough of this," said Mom. "Now get your presents and put them under the tree."

Peter ran off.

Henry stood still.

"Henry," said Mom. "Have you finished wrapping your Christmas presents?"

Yikes, thought Horrid Henry. What am I going to do now? The moment he'd been dreading for weeks had arrived.

"Henry! I'm not going to ask you again," said Mom. "Have you finished wrapping all your Christmas presents?"

"Yes!" bellowed Horrid Henry.

This was not entirely true. Henry had not finished wrapping his Christmas presents. In fact, he hadn't even started. The truth was, Henry had finished wrapping because he had no presents to wrap.

This was certainly *not* his fault. He *had* bought a few gifts, of course. He knew Peter would love the box of green Day-Glo slime. And if he didn't, well, he knew who to give it to. And Granny and Grandpa and Mom and Dad and Paul and Polly would have adored the big boxes of chocolates Henry had won at the school fair. Could he help it if the chocolates had called his name so loudly that he'd been forced to eat them all? And then Granny had been complaining about gaining weight. Surely it would have been very unkind to give her chocolate. And eating chocolate would have just made Pimply Paul's pimples worse. Henry'd done him a big favor eating that box.

And it was hardly Henry's fault when he'd needed extra goo for a raid on the Secret Club and Peter's present was the only stuff on hand? He'd *meant* to buy replacements. But he had so many things he needed to buy for himself that when he opened his skeleton bank to get out some cash for Christmas shopping, only 35 cents had rolled out.

"I've bought and wrapped all *my* presents, Mom," said Perfect Peter. "I've been saving my pocket money for months."

"Whoopee for you," said Henry.

"Henry, it's always better to give than to receive," said Peter.

Mom beamed. "Quite right, Peter."

"Says who?" growled Horrid Henry. "I'd much rather *get* presents."

"Don't be so horrid, Henry," said Mom.

"Don't be so selfish, Henry," said Dad.

Horrid Henry stuck out his tongue. Mom and Dad gasped.

"You horrid boy," said Mom.

"I just hope Santa Claus didn't see that," said Dad.

"Henry," said Peter, "Santa Claus

won't bring you any presents if you're
bad."

AAARRRGGHHH! Horrid Henry
sprang at Peter. He was a grizzly bear
guzzling a juicy morsel.

"AAAAIIEEE," wailed Peter. "Henry
pinched me."

"Henry! Go to your room," said
Mom.

"Fine!" screamed Horrid Henry,
stomping off and slamming the door.
Why did he get stuck with the world's
meanest and most horrible parents? *They*
certainly didn't deserve any presents.

Presents! Why couldn't he just *get* them? Why oh why did he have to *give* them? Giving other people presents was such a waste of his hard-earned money. Every time he gave a present it meant something he couldn't buy for himself. Good-bye chocolate. Good-bye comics. Good-bye Deluxe Goo-Shooter. And then, if you bought anything good, it was so horrible having to give it away. He'd practically cried having to give Ralph that Terminator Gladiator poster for his birthday. And the Mutant Max lunch box Mom made him give Kasim still made him gnash his teeth whenever he saw Kasim with it.

Now he was stuck, on Christmas Eve, with no money, and no presents to give anyone, deserving or not.

And then Henry had a wonderful, spectacular idea. It was so wonderful, and so spectacular, that he couldn't believe he hadn't thought of it before. Who said he had to *buy* presents? Didn't Mom and Dad always say it was the *thought* that counted? And oh boy was he thinking.

Granny was sure to love a Mutant Max comic. After all, who wouldn't? Then when she'd finished enjoying it, he could borrow it back. Horrid Henry rummaged under his bed and found a recent copy. In fact, it would be a shame if Grandpa got jealous of Granny's great present. Safer to give them each one, thought Henry, digging deep into his pile to find one with the fewest torn pages.

Now let's see, Mom and Dad. He could draw them a lovely picture. Nah, that would take too long. Even better, he could write them a poem.

Henry sat down at his desk, grabbed a pencil, and wrote:

Dear Old baldy Dad
Don't be sad
Be glad
Because you've had...
A very merry Christmas
Love from your lad,
Henry

Not bad, thought Henry. Not bad.
And so cheap! Now one for Mom.

Dear old wrinkly Mom
Don't be glum
Cause you've got a fat tum
And an even bigger bum
Ho ho ho hum
Love from your son,

Henry

Wow! It was hard finding so many
words to rhyme but he'd done it. And the
poem was nice and Christmasy with the
"ho ho ho." *Son* didn't rhyme but hope-
fully Mom wouldn't notice because she'd

be so thrilled with the rest of the poem.
When he was famous she'd be proud to
show off the poem her son had written
specially for her.

Now, Polly. Hmmm. She was always
squeaking and squealing
about dirt and dust. Maybe
a lovely kitchen sponge?
Or a rag she could use to
mop up after Vera? Or a
bucket to put over Pimply
Paul's head?

Wait. What about some
soap?

Horrid Henry ran into the
bathroom. Yes! There was a tempting bar
of blue soap going to waste in the soap
dish by the bathtub. True, it had been used
once or twice, but a bit of smoothing with
his fingers would sort that out. In fact,
Polly and Paul could share this present, it
was such a good one.

Whistling, Horrid Henry wrapped up
the soap in sparkling reindeer paper.
He was a genius. Why hadn't he ever
done this before? And a lovely rag from
under the sink would be perfect as a gag
for Vera.

That just left Peter and all his present
problems would be over. A piece of
chewing gum, only one careful owner? A
collage of candy wrappers that spelled out
Worm? The unused comb Peter had given
him last Christmas?

Aha. Peter loved bunnies.
What better present than a
picture of a bunny?

It was the work of
a few moments for
Henry to draw a
bunny and slash a
few blue lines across it
to color it in. Then he
signed his name in big

letters at the bottom. Maybe he should be a famous artist and not a poet when he grew up, he thought, admiring his handiwork. Henry had heard that artists got paid tons of cash just for stacking a few bricks or hurling paint at a white canvas. Being an artist sounded like a great job, since it left so much time for playing computer games.

Horrid Henry dumped his presents beneath the Christmas tree and sighed happily. This was one Christmas where he was sure to get a lot more than he gave. Whoopee! Who could ask for anything more?

3

HORRID HENRY'S AMBUSH

Christmas Eve
(just a few more hours to go!)

It was Christmas Eve at last. Every minute felt like an hour. Every hour felt like a year. How could Henry live until Christmas morning when he could get his hands on all his loot?

Mom and Dad were baking frantically in the kitchen.

Perfect Peter sat by the twinkling Christmas tree scratching out "Silent Night" over and over again on his cello.

"Can't you play something else?" snapped Henry.

"No," said Peter, sawing away. "This is the only Christmas carol I know. You can move if you don't like it."

"You move," said Henry.

Peter ignored him.

"Siiiiiiiii—lent Niiiiight," screeched the cello.

AAARRRGH.

Horrid Henry lay on the sofa with his fingers in his ears, double-checking his choices from the Toy Heaven catalog. Big red X's appeared on every page, to help you-know-who remember all the toys he absolutely had to have. Oh please, let everything he wanted leap from its pages and into Santa's sack. After all, what could be better than looking at a huge glittering stack of presents on Christmas morning, and knowing that they were all for you?

Oh please let this be the year when he finally got everything he wanted!

His letter to Santa Claus couldn't have been clearer.

Dear Santa Claus,

I want loads and loads and loads of cash, to make up for the puny amount you put in my stocking last year. And a Robomatic Supersonic Space Howler Deluxe plus attachments would be great too. I have asked for this before, you know!!! And the Terminator Gladiator fighting kit. I need lots more Day-Glo slime and comics and a Mutant Max poster and the new Zapatron Hip-Hop Dinosaur. This is your last chance.

Henry

P.S. Oranges are NOT presents!!!!!
P.P.S. Peter asked me to tell you to give me all his presents as he doesn't want any.

How hard could it be for Santa Claus to get this right? He'd asked for the Space Howler last year, and it never arrived. Instead, Henry got . . . vests. And handkerchiefs. And books. And clothes. And a—bleucccck—jigsaw puzzle and a jump rope and a tiny Waterblaster instead of the mega-sized one he'd specified. Yuck! Santa Claus obviously needed Henry's help.

Santa Claus is getting old and doddery, thought Henry. Maybe he hasn't got my letters. Maybe he's lost his reading glasses. Or—what a horrible thought—maybe he

was delivering Henry's presents by mistake
to some other Henry. Eeeek! Some yucky,
undeserving Henry was probably right
now this minute playing with Henry's
Terminator Gladiator sword, shield, axe,
and trident. And enjoying his Intergalactic
Samurai Gorillas. It was so unfair!

And then suddenly Henry had a
brilliant, spectacular idea. Why had he
never thought of this before? All his
present problems would be over.
Presents were far too important to leave
to Santa Claus. Since he couldn't be
trusted to bring the right gifts, Horrid
Henry had no choice. He would have to
ambush Santa Claus.

Yes!

He'd hold Santa Claus hostage with his
Goo-Shooter, while he rummaged in his
present sack for all the loot he was owed.
Maybe Henry would keep it all. Now
that would be fair.

Let's see, thought Horrid Henry. Santa Claus was bound to be a slippery character, so he'd need to booby-trap his bedroom. When you-know-who sneaked in to fill his stocking at the end of the bed, Henry could leap up and nab him. Santa Claus had a lot of explaining to do for all those years of stockings filled with oranges and walnuts instead of chocolate and cold hard cash.

So, how best to capture him?

Henry considered.

A bucket of water above the door.

A jump rope stretched tight across the entrance, guaranteed to trip up intruders.

A web of string crisscrossed from bedpost to door and threaded with bells to ensnare nighttime visitors.

And let's not forget strategically scattered whoopee cushions.

His plan was foolproof.

Loot, here I come, thought Horrid Henry.

Horrid Henry sat up in bed, his Goo-
Shooter aimed at the half-open door
where a bucket of water balanced. All

his traps were laid. No one was getting in without Henry knowing about it. Any minute now, he'd catch Santa Claus and make him pay up.

Henry waited. And waited. And waited. His eyes started to feel heavy and he closed them for a moment.

There was a rustling at Henry's door.

Oh my gosh, this was it! Henry lay down and pretended to be asleep.

Cr-eeeek.
Cr-eeeek.

Horrid Henry reached for his Goo-Shooter.

A huge shape loomed in the doorway. Henry braced himself to attack.

"Doesn't he look sweet when he's asleep?" whispered the shape.

"What a little snugglechops," whispered another.

Sweet? Snugglechops?

Horrid Henry's fingers itched to let
Mom and Dad have it with both barrels.

POW!

Splat!

Henry could see it now. Mom covered
in green goo. Dad covered in green goo.
Mom and Dad snatching the Goo-Shooter
and wrecking all his plans and throwing

out all his presents and banning him from TV forever . . . hmmm. His fingers felt a little less itchy.

Henry lowered his Goo-Shooter. The bucket of water wobbled above the door.

Yikes! What if Mom and Dad stepped into his Santa traps? All his hard work—ruined.

"I'm awake," snarled Henry.

The shapes stepped back. The water stopped wobbling.

"Go to sleep!" hissed Mom.

"Go to sleep!" hissed Dad.

"What are you doing here?" demanded Henry.

"Checking on you," said Mom. "Now go to sleep or Santa Claus will never come."

He'd better, thought Henry.

Horrid Henry woke with a jolt. AAARRGGH! He'd fallen asleep. How

could he? Panting and gasping Henry
switched on the light. Phew. His traps
were intact. His stocking was empty.
Santa Claus hadn't been yet.

Wow, was that lucky. That was incredibly
lucky. Henry lay back, his heart pounding.

And then Horrid Henry had a terrible
thought.

What if Santa Claus had decided to be
spiteful and *avoid* Henry's bedroom this
year? Or what if he'd played a sneaky
trick on Henry and filled a stocking
downstairs instead?

Nah. No way.

But wait. When Santa Claus came to
Rude Ralph's house he always filled the
stockings downstairs. Now Henry came
to think of it, Moody Margaret always left
her stocking downstairs too, hanging from
the fireplace, not from the end of her bed,
like Henry did.

Horrid Henry looked at the clock.

It was past midnight. Mom and Dad had forbidden him to go downstairs till morning, on pain of having all his presents taken away and no TV all day.

But this was an emergency. He'd creep downstairs, take a quick peek to make sure he hadn't missed Santa Claus, then be back in bed in a jiffy.

No one will ever know, thought Horrid Henry.

Henry tiptoed around the whoopee cushions, leaped over the crisscross threads, stepped over the jump rope and carefully squeezed through his door so as not to disturb the bucket of water. Then he crept downstairs.

Sneak
   Sneak
      Sneak

Horrid Henry shone his flashlight over the living room. Santa Claus hadn't been. The room was exactly as he'd left it that evening.

Except for one thing. Henry's light illuminated the Christmas tree, heavy with chocolate Santas and chocolate bells and chocolate reindeer. Mom and Dad must have hung them on the tree after he'd gone to bed.

Horrid Henry looked at the chocolates cluttering up the Christmas tree. Shame, thought Horrid Henry, the way those chocolates spoil the view of all those lovely decorations. You could barely see the baubles and tinsel he and Peter had worked so hard to put on.

"Hi, Henry," said the chocolate Santas. "Don't you want to eat us?"

"Go on, Henry," said the chocolate bells. "You know you want to."

"What are you waiting for, Henry?" urged the chocolate reindeer.

What indeed? After all, it *was* Christmas.

Henry took a chocolate Santa or three from the side, and then another two from the back. Mmm, boy, was that great chocolate, he thought, stuffing them into his mouth.

Oops. Now the chocolate Santas looked a little unbalanced.

Better take a few from the front and from the other side, to even it up, thought Henry. Then no one will notice there are a few chocolates missing.

Henry gobbled and gorged and guzzled. Wow, were those chocolates yummy!!!

The tree looks a bit bare, thought Henry a little while later. Mom had such eagle eyes she might notice that a few— well, all—of the chocolates were missing. He'd better hide all those gaps with a

few extra baubles. And, while he was
improving the tree, he could swap that
stupid fairy for Terminator Gladiator.

Henry piled extra decorations onto the
branches. Soon the Christmas tree was so
covered in baubles and tinsel there
was barely a hint of green. No one
would notice the missing chocolates.
Then Henry stood on a chair, dumped
the fairy, and, standing on his tippy-tippy
toes, hung Terminator Gladiator at the
top where he belonged.

Perfect, thought Horrid Henry, jumping off the chair and stepping back to admire his work. Absolutely perfect.  Thanks to me this is the best tree ever.

There was a terrible creaking sound. Then another. Then suddenly . . .

CRASH!

The Christmas tree toppled over.

Horrid Henry's heart stopped.

Upstairs he could hear Mom and Dad
stirring.

"Hey! Who's down there?" shouted Dad.

RUN!!! thought Horrid Henry. Run
for your life!!

Horrid Henry ran like he had never run
before, up the stairs to his room before
Mom and Dad could catch him. Oh please
let him get there in time. His parents'

bedroom door opened just as Henry dashed inside his room. He'd made it. He was safe.

SPLASH! The bucket of water spilled all over him.

TRIP! Horrid Henry fell over the jump rope.

CRASH! SMASH!
RING! RING! jangled the bells.
PLLLLLLL!
belched the whoopee cushions.

"What is going on in here?" shrieked Mom, glaring.

"Nothing," said Horrid Henry, as he lay sprawled on the floor soaking wet and tangled up in threads and wires and rope. "I heard a noise downstairs so I got up to check," he added innocently.

"Tree's fallen over," called Dad. "Must have been overloaded. Don't worry, I'll fix it."

"Get back to bed, Henry," said Mom wearily. "And don't touch your stocking till morning."

Henry looked. And gasped. His stocking was stuffed and bulging. That mean old sneak, thought Horrid Henry indignantly. How did he do it? How had he escaped the traps?

Watch out Santa Claus, thought Horrid Henry. I'll get you next year.

4

HORRID HENRY'S CHRISTMAS LUNCH

December 25th
(at last!)

"Oh, handkerchiefs, just what I wanted," said Perfect Peter. "Thank you *so* much."

"Not handkerchiefs *again*," moaned Horrid Henry, throwing the hankies aside and ripping the paper off the next present in his pile.

"Don't tear the wrapping paper!" squeaked Perfect Peter.

Horrid Henry ripped open the present and groaned.

Yuck (a pen, pencil, and ruler). Yuck (a dictionary). Yuck (gloves). OK ($15—should have been a lot more). Eeew (a pink bow tie from Aunt Ruby). Eeew (mints). Yum (huge tin of chocolates). Good (five more knights for his army). Very good (a subscription to Gross-Out Fan Club) . . .

And (very very good) a Terminator Gladiator trident . . . and . . .

And . . . where was the rest?

"Is that it?" shrieked Henry.

"You haven't opened my present, Henry," said Peter. "I hope you like it."

Horrid Henry tore off the wrapping. It was a Manners with Maggie calendar.

"Ugh, gross," said Henry. "No thank you."

"Henry!" said Mom. "That's no way to receive a present."

"I don't care," moaned Horrid Henry. "Where's my Zapatron Hip-Hop dinosaur? And where's the rest of the Terminator Gladiator fighting kit? I wanted everything, not just the trident."

"Maybe next year," said Mom.

"But I want it now!" howled Henry.

"Henry, you know that 'I want doesn't get'," said Peter. "Isn't that right, Mom?"

"It certainly is," said Mom. "And I haven't heard you say thank you, Henry."

Horrid Henry glared at Peter and sprang. He was a hornet stinging a worm to death.

"WAAAAAAH!" wailed Peter.

"Henry! Stop it or—"

Ding! Dong!

"They're here!" shouted Horrid Henry, leaping up and abandoning his prey. "That means more presents!"

"Wait, Henry," said Mom.

But too late. Henry raced to the door and flung it open.

There stood Granny and Grandpa, Prissy Polly, Pimply Paul, and Vomiting Vera.

"Gimme my presents!" he shrieked, snatching a bag of brightly wrapped gifts out of Granny's hand and spilling them on the floor. Now, where were the ones with his name on them?

"Merry Christmas, everyone," said Mom brightly. "Henry, don't be rude."

"I'm not being rude," said Henry. "I just want my presents. Great, money!" said

Henry, beaming. "Thanks, Granny! But couldn't you add a few dollars and—"

"Henry, don't be horrid!" snapped Dad.

"Let the guests take off their coats," said Mom.

"Bleeeeech," said Vomiting Vera, throwing up on Paul.

"Eeeeek," said Polly.

All the grown-ups gathered in the living room to open their gifts.

"Peter, thank you so much for the perfume, it's my favorite," said Granny.

"I know," said Peter.

"And what a lovely comic, Henry," said Granny. "Mutant Max is my . . . um . . . favorite."

"Thank you, Henry," said Grandpa. "This comic looks very . . . interesting."

"I'll have it back when you've finished with it," said Henry.

"Henry!" said Mom, glaring.

For some reason Polly didn't look delighted with her present.

"Eeeek!" squeaked Polly. "This soap has . . . hairs in it." She pulled out a long black one.

"That came free," said Horrid Henry.

"We're getting you toothpaste next year, you little brat," muttered Pimply Paul under his breath.

Honestly, there was no pleasing some people, thought Horrid Henry indignantly. He'd given Paul a great bar of soap, and he didn't seem thrilled. So much for it's the thought that counts.

"A poem," said Mom. "Henry, how lovely."

"Read it out loud," said Grandpa.

"Dear old wrinkly Mom
Don't be glum
'Cause you've got a fat tum
And an even bigger..."

"Maybe later," said Mom.

"Another poem," said Dad. "Great!"

"Let's hear it," said Granny.

"Dear old baldy Dad—

. . . and so forth," said Dad, folding Henry's poem quickly.

"Oh," said Polly, staring at the crystal frog vase Mom and Dad had given her.

"How funny. This looks just like the vase *I* gave Aunt Ruby for Christmas last year."

"What a coincidence," said Mom, blushing bright red.

"Great minds think alike," said Dad quickly.

Dad gave Mom an iron.

70

"Oh, an iron, just what I always wanted," said Mom.

Mom gave Dad oven gloves.

"Oh, oven gloves, just what I always wanted," said Dad.

Pimply Paul gave Prissy Polly a huge power drill.

"Eeeek," squealed Polly. "What's this?"

"Oh, that's the Megawatt Superduper Drill-o-matic 670 XM3," said Paul, "and just wait till you see the attachments. You're getting those for your birthday."

"Oh," said Polly.

Granny gave Grandpa a lovely mug to put his false teeth in.

Grandpa gave Granny a shower cap and a jumbo pack of dusters.

"What super presents!" said Mom.

"Yes," said Perfect Peter. "I loved every single one of my presents, especially the oranges and walnuts in my stocking."

"I didn't," said Horrid Henry.

"Henry, don't be horrid," said Dad. "Who'd like a mince pie?"

"Are they homemade or from the store?" asked Henry.

"Homemade of course," said Dad.

"Gross," said Henry.

"Ooh," said Polly. "No, Vera!" she squealed as Vera vomited all over the plate.

"Never mind," said Mom tightly. "There's more in the kitchen."

Horrid Henry was bored. Horrid Henry was fed up. The presents had all been opened. His parents had made him go on a long, boring walk. Dad had confiscated his Terminator trident when he had speared Peter with it.

So, what now?

Grandpa was sitting in the armchair with his pipe, snoring, his tinsel crown slipping over his face.

Prissy Polly and Pimply Paul were squabbling over whose turn it was to change Vera's stinky diaper.

"Eeeek," said Polly. "I did it last."

"I did," said Paul.

"WAAAAAAAAA!" wailed Vomiting Vera.

Perfect Peter was watching Sammy the Snail slithering about on TV.

Horrid Henry snatched the remote and switched channels.

"Hey, I was watching that!" protested Peter.

"Tough," said Henry.

Let's see, what was on? "Tra la la la . . ." Ick! Daffy and her Dancing Daisies.

"Wait! I want to watch!" wailed Peter.

Click. ". . . And the tension builds as
the judges compare tomatoes grown . . ."
Click! " . . . Wish you a Merry Christmas,
we wish you . . ." Click! "Chartres
Cathedral is one of the wonders of . . . "
Click! "HA HA HA HA HA HA HA HA."
Opera! Click! Why was there nothing good
on TV? Just a baby
movie about singing
cars he'd
seen a
million
times
already.
"I'm
bored,"
moaned

Henry. "And I'm starving." He wan-
dered into the kitchen, which looked
like a hurricane had swept through.

"When's lunch? I thought we were
eating at two. I'm starving."

"Soon," said Mom. She looked a little

frazzled. "There's been a little problem with the oven."

"So when's lunch?" bellowed Horrid Henry.

"When it's ready!" bellowed Dad.

Henry waited. And waited. And waited.

"When's lunch?" asked Polly.

"When's lunch?" asked Paul.

"When's lunch?" asked Peter.

"As soon as the turkey is cooked," said Dad. He peeked into the oven. He poked the turkey. Then he went pale.

"It's hardly cooked," he whispered.

"Check the temperature," said Granny. Dad checked.

"Oops," said Dad.

"Never mind, we can start with the sprouts," said Mom cheerfully.

"That's not the right way to do sprouts," said Granny. "You're peeling too many of the leaves off."

76

"Yes, Mother," said Dad.

"That's not the right way to make gravy," said Granny.

"Yes, Mother," said Dad.

"That's not the right way to make stuffing," said Granny.

"Yes, Mother," said Dad.

"That's not the right way to roast potatoes," said Granny.

"Mother!" yelped Dad. "Leave me alone!"

"Don't be horrid," said Granny.

"I'm not being horrid," said Dad.

"Come along, Granny, let's get you a nice drink and leave the chef on his own," said Mom, steering Granny firmly toward the living room. Then she stopped.

"Is something burning?" asked Mom, sniffing.

Dad checked the oven.

"Not in here."

There was a shriek from the living room.

"It's Grandpa!" shouted Perfect Peter.

Everyone ran in.

There was Grandpa, asleep in his chair. A thin column of black smoke rose from

the arms. His paper crown, drooping over his pipe, was smoking.

"Whh..whh?" mumbled Grandpa, as Mom whacked him with her broom. "AAARRGH!" he gurgled as Dad threw water over him.

"When's lunch?" screamed Horrid Henry.

"When it's ready," screamed Dad.

★ ★ ★

It was dark when Henry's family finally sat down to Christmas lunch. Henry's tummy was rumbling so loudly with hunger he thought the walls would cave in. Henry and Peter made a dash to grab the seat against the wall, furthest from the kitchen.

"Get off!" shouted Henry.

"It's my turn to sit here," wailed Peter.

"Mine!"

"Mine!"

Slap!

Slap!

"WAAAAAAAAAAA!" screeched Henry.

"WAAAAAAAAAAAA!" wailed Peter.

"Quiet!" screamed Dad.

Mom brought in fresh holly and ivy to decorate the table.

"Lovely," said Mom, placing the boughs all along the center.

"Very festive," said Granny.

"I'm starving!" wailed Horrid Henry. "This isn't Christmas lunch, it's Christmas dinner."

"Shhh," said Grandpa.

The turkey was finally cooked. There were platefuls of stuffing, sprouts, cranberries, gravy, and peas.

"Smells good," said Granny.

"Mmmm, boy," said Grandpa. "What a feast."

Horrid Henry was so hungry he could eat the tablecloth.

"Come on, let's eat!" he said.

"Hold on, I'll just get the roast potatoes," said Dad. Wearing his new oven gloves, he carried in the steaming hot potatoes in a glass roasting dish, and set it in the middle of the table.

"*Voila!*" said Dad. "Now, who wants dark meat and who . . ."

"What's that crawling . . . aaaarrrghh!" screamed Polly. "There are spiders every-where!"

Millions of tiny spiders
were pouring from the
holly and crawling all
over the table and the
food.

"Don't panic!"
shouted Pimply
Paul, leaping
from his chair,
"I know what to do,
we just—"

But before
he could do
anything the glass dish with the roasted
potatoes exploded.

CRASH!

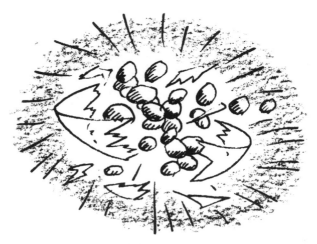

SMASH!

"EEEEEKK!" screamed Polly.

Everyone stared at the slivers of glass glistening all over the table and the food.

Dad sank down in his chair and covered his eyes.

"Where are we going to get more food?" whispered Mom.

"I don't know," muttered Dad.

"I know," said Horrid Henry, "let's start with Christmas pudding and defrost some pizzas."

Dad opened his eyes.

Mom opened her eyes.

"That," said Dad, "is a brilliant idea."

"I really hanker for some pizza," said Grandpa.

"Me too," said Granny.

Henry beamed. It wasn't often his ideas were recognized for their brilliance.

"Merry Christmas everyone," said Horrid Henry. "Merry Christmas."

Acknowledgments

My thanks to Susie Boyt, Amanda Craig, Judith Elliott, Fiona Kennedy and Kate Saunders for sharing their Christmas disaster stories with me.

Horrid Henry's
Family, Friends, and Enemies

Aerobic Al

Anxious Andrew

Aunt Ruby...

Beefy Bert........................

Bossy Bill...

Brainy Brian

Clever Clare........................

Dad...

Dizzy Dave........................

Fiery Fiona

Horrid Henry's Family, Friends, and Enemies

...............Fluffy the cat

Goody-Goody Gordon

Gorgeous Gurinder

............................Grandpa

..................Granny

Great Aunt Greta

Greedy Graham

..................................Inky Ian

..........................Jazzy Jim

................................Jolly Josh

Jumpy Jeffrey

Kind Kasim

Kung-Fu Kate

Lazy Linda

Lisping Lilly..

Magic Martha

Miss Battle-Axe...............

Miss Lovely...

Miss Thumper...................

Miss Tutu...

Mom....................................

Moody Margaret............................

Mr. Nerdon........................

Mrs. Oddbod..................................

Horrid Henry's Family, Friends, and Enemies

New Nick

Perfect Peter

Pimply Paul

Prissy Polly

Rabid Rebecca

Rude Ralph

Singing Soraya

Soggy Sid

Sour Susan

Stuck-up Steve

Tidy Ted

Tough Toby

Vain Violet................................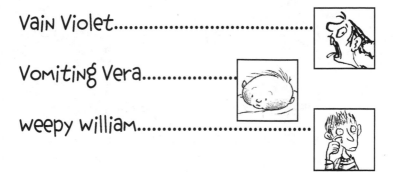

Vomiting Vera..................

weepy william.................................

Visit
www.HorridHenry.com
for more fun!

The HORRID HENRY books
by Francesca Simon

Illustrated by Tony Ross

Each book contains four stories

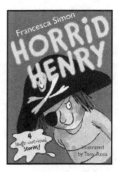

HORRID HENRY

Henry is dragged to dancing class against his will; vies with Moody Margaret to make the yuckiest Glop; goes camping; and tries to be good like Perfect Peter—but not for long.

HORRID HENRY TRICKS THE TOOTH FAIRY

Horrid Henry tries to trick the Tooth Fairy into giving him more money; sends Moody Margaret packing; causes his teachers to run screaming from school; and single-handedly wrecks a wedding.

HORRID HENRY and THE MEGA-MEAN TIME MACHINE

Horrid Henry reluctantly goes for a hike; builds a time machine and convinces Perfect Peter that boys wear dresses in the future; Perfect Peter plays one of the worst tricks ever on his brother; and Henry's aunt takes the family to a fancy restaurant, so his parents bribe him to behave.

HORRID HENRY'S STINKBOMB

Horrid Henry uses a stinkbomb as a toxic weapon in his long-running war with Moody Margaret; uses all his tricks to win the school reading competition; goes for a sleepover and retreats in horror when he finds that other people's houses aren't always as nice as his own; and has the joy of seeing Miss Battle-Axe in hot water with the principle when he knows it was all his fault.

HORRID HENRY AND THE MUMMY'S CURSE

Horrid Henry indulges his favorite hobby—collecting Gizmos; has a bad time with his spelling homework; starts a rumor that there's a shark in the pool; and spooks Perfect Peter with the mummy's curse.

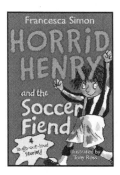

HORRiD HENRY AND THE SOCCER FiEND

Horrid Henry reads Perfect Peter's diary and improves it; goes shopping with Mom and tries to make her buy him some really nice new sneakers; is horrified when his old enemy Bossy Bill turns up at school; and tries by any means, to win the class soccer match.

HORRID HENRY AND THE SCARY SITTER

Horrid Henry encounters the worst babysitter in the world; traumatizes his parents on a long car trip; is banned from trick-or-treating at Halloween; and emerges victorious from a raid on Moody Margaret's Secret Club.

About the Author

Photo: Francesco Guidicini

Francesca Simon spent her childhood on the beach in California and then went to Yale and Oxford Universities to study medieval history and literature. She now lives in London with her family. She has written over forty-five books and won the Children's Book of the Year in 2008 at the Galaxy British Book Awards for *Horrid Henry and the Abominable Snowman*.